© 2006 The Walt Disney Company
Published by Hachette Partworks Ltd
ISBN: 978-1-906965-10-5
Date of Printing: December 2008
Printed in Singapore by Tien Wah Press

Far beneath the ocean's surface lived the
enchanting merpeople. Their ruler was King Triton.
He had seven daughters, and Ariel, his youngest,
loved to sing.

Triton was so proud of Ariel's voice that he had
planned a royal concert. All the merpeople would be
there. And Sebastian, the court composer, was really
looking forward to conducting his new symphony
before the King.

The day of the concert finally arrived. To introduce Ariel, her six sisters swam in front of a large seashell. When Sebastian gave the sign, they opened the shell. But instead of Ariel appearing, the shell was empty!

"ARIEL!"
King Triton yelled.

But Ariel didn't hear him. She had forgotten all about the royal concert and was far away from the royal palace.

Ariel and her best friend, Flounder, spent most of their time exploring sunken shipwrecks. Whenever they found a small human treasure, Ariel added it to her hidden collection.

On this particular day, Ariel and Flounder were exploring an old shipwreck.

Flounder thought the place was
scary, but Ariel was very excited. She
even found an object she had never
seen before – a fork.

"What is it?" Flounder asked.

"I don't know," replied Ariel excitedly.
"But I bet Scuttle will!"

So the two
of them swam
to the water's
surface to find
Ariel's friend – a
seagull named
Scuttle.

Ariel showed Scuttle her new treasure.

"I do believe this is a *dinglehopper*," said Scuttle. "Humans use these little babies to straighten their hair out."

Just then Ariel remembered that she was supposed to sing at the concert, and she and Flounder hurried home.

Back at the palace, King Triton was so angry that he ordered Sebastian to follow Ariel and keep her out of trouble.

Later that day, a huge shadow darkened the
waters above her secret cave.
"What do you suppose... ?" began Ariel.
Before Sebastian could stop
her, Ariel swam to the
surface and discovered
that the shadow was
actually a ship!

Ariel pulled herself to the edge of the deck, where she saw humans. She was fascinated by the handsome young man the others called Prince Eric. He was looking at his birthday present: a huge, foolish statue of himself.

"Huh," said Eric. "It's really... something."

"Hurricane a-comin'!" a sailor suddenly shouted. The ship began to pitch and roll in the storm. Then a bolt of lightning struck the mast and set the ship on fire.

"Look out!" yelled Eric as the ship hit some tall rocks. The men jumped into their lifeboats. But before Eric could leap from the deck, an explosion knocked him unconscious and threw him into the sea.

Ariel dived into the fiery debris to save Eric. Using all her strength, she swam with him towards shore and pulled him out onto the sand.

"Is he dead?" Ariel asked.

"It's hard to say," replied Scuttle, as he listened for Eric's heartbeat to see if the Prince was alive. Unfortunately, Scuttle was listening to Eric's foot!

But Ariel saw that he was breathing and sang softly to him.

When Ariel heard voices
approaching, she quickly
disappeared into the water.
Then Ariel and her friends
watched from a large rock.

Eric had never seen Ariel.
He had only heard her
beautiful voice. But
Ariel had fallen in
love with him!

After Ariel returned to her cave, her
father showed up. Without meaning to,
Sebastian told the king that Ariel was in
love – with a human!

Triton was furious. "Contact between the
human world and the merworld is strictly
forbidden!" he thundered.

"Daddy, I love him!" Ariel
protested.

Stunned, Triton raised
his trident and shattered
all of Ariel's special
human treasures.

After her father left, Ariel was very unhappy.
Then two evil eels, Flotsam and Jetsam,
slithered out from behind some rocks.

"Don't be scared," said Jetsam.
"We represent someone who can
help. Someone who can make all
your dreams come true."

Before she knew it, Ariel was
inside the deep, dark cave of Ursula
the sea witch!

The sea witch offered to help Ariel visit the Prince – for a fee.

"Now," said Ursula, "here's the deal: I'll make you a potion that will turn you into a human for three days. If the Prince kisses you before sunset on the third day, you'll remain human permanently."

"But if he doesn't," Ursula added, "you'll turn back into a mermaid, and you'll belong to me!"

Like all mean witches, Ursula wanted something in return. "What I want from you is your voice!" Ursula exclaimed. Then Ursula recited a magical spell and a mist rose up, surrounding Ariel. Reluctantly, Ariel signed her name to Ursula's "deal".

The little mermaid's voice was sucked from her throat into a shell necklace around Ursula's neck. Suddenly, Ariel couldn't talk or sing. Then a bright light flashed, and Ariel's tail was transformed into two legs!

Ariel could no longer live underwater. Sebastian and Flounder helped her to the surface so that she could breathe. Ariel stared with wonder at her legs!

Since the storm, Prince Eric had searched every day for the girl who saved him. "That voice – I can't get it out of my head," he told his dog, Max.

When Eric saw Ariel, he thought he had found his rescuer. But because she couldn't speak, he said, "You can't be who I thought you were."

Still, Eric invited her for dinner at his castle. That night, Ariel found a *dinglehopper* next to her plate. Not knowing any better, she started combing her hair with it!

The next day, Eric took Ariel on a
romantic boat ride in a sparkling lagoon.
They had a wonderful time.

But just as the Prince was about to kiss
Ariel – SPLASH! – Flotsam and Jetsam
tipped over the rowboat!

Ursula saw it all through her magic bubble.

"Nice work, boys," she said. "That was a close one. Too close."

Worried that the Prince would kiss Ariel before sunset the next day, Ursula came up with a wicked plan.

She turned herself into a beautiful young woman and called herself Vanessa. With Ariel's voice locked inside the shell necklace, Ursula sounded just like Ariel!

When Ursula walked near Eric's castle, the Prince thought she was his rescuer. She sang with the same beautiful voice of the girl who had pulled him from the sea.

The sea witch quickly put a spell
on Eric, and he decided to marry her
right away.

Ariel was brokenhearted when
she heard the news. But there was
nothing Ariel could do. She didn't
know that Vanessa was really Ursula
in disguise.

On the day of the wedding, Ariel, Flounder
and Sebastian were near the water's edge when
Scuttle arrived.

"The Prince is marrying the sea witch in
disguise!" announced Scuttle.

Ariel and her friends hurried to the ship.
In the middle of the wedding, a group of birds
attacked the sea witch. Then Scuttle snatched
away the shell necklace.

The necklace fell onto the deck. A golden mist streamed from the broken shell and into Ariel's throat.

Overwhelmed with joy, Ariel started to sing, and Eric rushed towards her to kiss her.

"You're too late!" bragged Ursula, who turned back into her mean self.

Ariel tried to run, but she fell because she was a mermaid again. Ursula dragged helpless Ariel back into the sea.

Suddenly
Triton emerged
from the depths and
confronted the sea witch.
"Let her go!" he demanded.
"Not a chance, Triton!" said Ursula.
"We made a deal." Ursula showed him the
golden scroll signed by Ariel.

Without thinking twice, King Triton pointed his
trident at the scroll and changed Ariel's name into
his own. He was now Ursula's prisoner, and Ariel
was free.

"At last!" Ursula cried and grabbed the golden
trident. Now she was ruler of all the seas! Ursula
grew to an enormous size.

With the trident, Ursula stirred the water into a raging whirlpool and even raised a ship from the bottom of the sea.

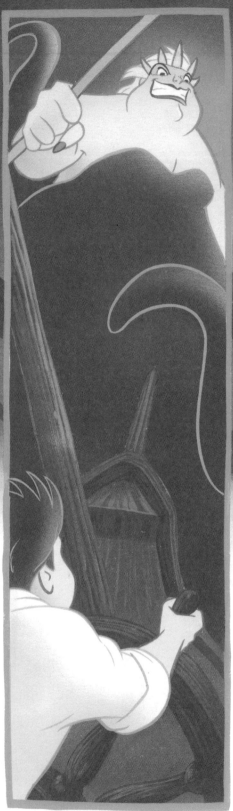

Eric climbed aboard
and steered the ship
straight towards the
sea witch.

"AAAAHHH!" Ursula screamed in pain when the ship struck her. Within seconds only a few tentacles were left floating around the ship.

The sea witch's spell was broken, and Triton retrieved his trident. He was once again ruler of the underwater world.

With wicked
Ursula gone,
everything returned to
normal in King Triton's
undersea kingdom. But now
that Ariel was a mermaid again, she
couldn't be with her beloved Prince Eric.

King Triton saw how unhappy Ariel was and
used his magic powers to give her legs. Flounder
and Sebastian knew they would miss her, but they
also knew she would be happiest on land with Eric.

Soon Prince
Eric and Ariel
were married, and
they lived happily
ever after.